To all of the poets lurking in the woods, preparing to ambush the world with their poems.
—B.R.

For Emerson, our boy with a kind heart. Keep exploring. Keep writing.
—K&K

Text copyright © 2021 Bob Raczka
Illustration copyright © 2021 by Kevin & Kristen Howdeshell
Book design by Melissa Nelson Greenberg

Library of Congress Cataloging-in-Publication Data available

ISBN: 978-1-951836-09-2

Printed in China

10 9 8 7 6 5 4 3 2 1

Cameron Kids is an imprint of Cameron + Company

Cameron + Company
Petaluma, California
www.cameronbooks.com

THE POET
OF PINEY WOODS

by Bob Raczka • art by Kevin & Kristen Howdeshell

cameron kids

Monarchs. Wolf creeps,
sees Rabbit leap.
Wolf can't hold sneeze.
Wings fly. Fur flees.

Berries. Wolf snoops.
Cub chomps and scoops.

Twig snaps. Cub hears,
then . . . disappears.

Round pond. Wolf sneaks.
Frog croaks, puffs cheeks.

Wolf smiles. Teeth flash.
Frog sees Wolf. Splash!

Sundown. Wolf's lair.
Dinner? Sliced pears.
Peaceful. Poem time.
Wolf thinks, inks rhymes.

Daybreak. Bright sun.
Wolf wakes. Poems done.
He wants to share
his words. But where?

Wolf posts his lines
upon a pine.
They draw a crowd,
who read out loud:

Bunny & Butterfly

Flash, dip,
dash, skip.
Loop, dive,
swoop, jive.
Grab it,
Rabbit!
Got?
Not.

Black Bear-ies

Cute black
fruit snack.
Tiny.
Shiny.
Pick some,
lick thumbs.
Cub
grub.

Pond Poem

Oak - clogged.
Fog - cloaked.
Soaked log.
Frog croaks.
makes a
splash.
Takes a
bath.

"We love these words!"
tweet all the birds.
"Who wrote them though?"
inquires Doe.

Beyond the pines,
a voice: "They're mine."
The creatures, scared,
reply, "Who's there?"

Bunny & Butterfly

Flash, dip,
dash, skip.
Loop, dive,
swoop, jive.
Grab it,
Rabbit!
Got?
Not.

Black Bear-ies

Cute black
fruit snack.
Tiny.
Shiny!
Pick some,
lick thumbs.
Cub
grub.

Pond Poem
Oak-clogged.
Fog-cloaked.
Soaked log.
Frog croaks.
Makes a
splash.
Takes a
bath.

When Wolf appears,
they freeze in fear.
Then, being prey,
they run away.

Wolf sits alone
among the cones
of pine and sighs,
"I'm not surprised."

"A wolf, I am,
and so they scram.
Yet I don't eat
a bite of meat."

"No meat, you say?"
The voice is Jay.
"You should have said
before they fled."

Jay cries, "COME BACK!
YOU WON'T BE SNACKS!"
The creatures hear
and reappear.

"Please don't be scared,"
says Wolf, "I swear
I never bite.
I'd rather write."

"But what about
your toothy snout?"
Wolf clears the air:
"For eating pears."

The creatures pause,
and then . . . applause.
His face a grin,
Wolf soaks it in.

They laugh and share
great plates of pears
as Wolf recites
into the night.

Now moonlight shines
upon the pines,
especially
the "poet tree."